# *Not Worth Killing*

Thunderstorms and murder. Four bodies, all competitive socialites. What did they have in common, other than almost identical, empty lives, that someone killed them for?

# Contents

# About the author

CD Moulton has traveled extensively over much of the world both in the music business, where he was a rock guitarist, songwriter and arranger and in an import/export business. He has been everything from a bar owner to auto salvage (junkyard) manager, longshoreman to high steel worker, orchid grower to landscaper, tropical fish farmer to commercial fisherman. He started writing books in 1983 and has published more than 350 books as of January 1, 2023. His most popular books to date are about research with orchids, though much of his science fiction and fantasy work has proven popular. He wrote the CD Grimes, PI series, and the Det. Nick Storie series, Clint Faraday series, and many other works.

He now resides in Gualaca, Chiriqui, Panamá, where he writes books, plays music with friends, does research with orchids and medicinal plants. He has lately become involved in fighting for the rights of the indigenous people, who are among his closest friends, and in fighting the extreme corruption in the courts and police in Panamá.

He offers the free e-book, *Fading Paradise*, that explains what he has been through because of the corruption.

CD is the discoverer of the Chadam Protocol for curing cancer.

Facebook page Ambrosia peruviana for cancer.

Anne Milsap stared out the window at the driving rain. The lightning streaks were a bit too bright and close to be pretty. She usually liked thunderstorms, but this one was a bit overdone, to her way of thinking.

She sighed and turned back into the room. She could use another cup of hot coffee. This one did bring a chill.

6:35. More coffee and she wouldn't sleep.

Damn! That one was close! Loud and rolling.

She went into the kitchen to plug in the coffee maker. A couple of cinnamon rolls on the plate. Might as well add another couple of ounces so she could spend an extra hour working it off.

Life sucks. Then you die and go to Hell for all your trying to live like a decent person.

She went into the dark living room to turn on the stereo. Might as well have something to lighten things. She certainly wouldn't want to go out tonight. She was holding her own with her "friends" in the competition bit. She could use a bit of rest from the rat-race where women were so naturally competitive.

Truth be told, she was disappointed most of the time with the ones who were supposed to be the prizes. They were so sold on themselves they were worthless in a real relationship.

Why did nature come up with this system where women had to compete, even when they didn't want to? Why did, every time one of her regular friends find some guy who seemed special, she get that compulsion to take him away? It was silly – but it also was. That's life!

*Dark Side of the Moon.* Lighten the mood? Gimme a break!

Why was the door open? She never....


Barbara "Barbs" Lakehurst looked out at the sky.

What she could see of it. The cover was pretty much complete.

That would pretty much screw up her day and night! Shit!

Work your ass off to get noticed by someone like Kyle Kohnrad, then it rains on your parade when you finally get to him! Shit!

She had just *known* he would be someone she had to have the minute Ginger Parker introduced him. If there was one person in their little group who she could always best in that area, it was Ginger!

If it would just let up a little so she could get her hair to looking less like a rat nest she could hope to get into a better mood.

7:40 and no sign of a letup. Damn it all to Hell!

What was than noise on the terrace? If that damned alley cat the Drews let roam all over everybody's place but theirs was out there it was going to have an accident! This was the perfect time and she was in the perfect mood to see if cats could fly. Eight stories? See if the damned thing would land on its feet!

She charged out onto the terrace. The noise was from the right, over by the potted palm.

What.!?!


Ginger Parker studied the face in her mirror.

So. She was no raving beauty. A little makeup here and there, tailored clothes. A bit of padding.

Rain. It helped her, while it made a mess out of so many others. It affected the light and it let her wear things that set off the few better points.

The L'Ouvuer rain suit. Slick shiny plastic. White and black. A red purse and umbrella. The only thing that could possibly make pearls acceptable for anyone less than forty to wear.

The D'Or sunglasses. Mysterious. Raincoat and sunglasses.

The Guchi boots. The ones with the ... the red

ones, so she would be red over and under and black and white between.

The Jaguar. She would damned well be the glamour queen tonight! This was her milieu all the way. Eat your hearts out, bitches! Most nights are made for your games. Tonight's made for mine! We'll just see who comes out on top of this one!

She looked at the clock. 8:14. She had time to get this one right.

When the moment came, she slinked out to the door, told Carol she would be home when she got home, so lock the place when she went off work. She went out along the covered walk to the garage. She was unlocking the Jag when there was a noise behind her. She started to turn....

Gladys Rolf looked out at the rain and sighed. She waited for 8:30 to decide if she wanted to go anywhere. It was going to rain on, so to hell with it. She could use one or two nights without parties and assholes trying to pick her up like she was some kind of bar whore.

She bought that DVD set of four Leslie Neilson comedies. He played the perfect inept lover – which she felt 99% of the men she met were. For him to be able to play that role meant he knew it was all the stupid things. That made it comedy.

It also meant he knew the things that were real technique. She'd bet he was a fantastic lover, in reality. It wouldn't be like the regular thing with him. She could take any man from any woman with a coy look. Him, he would mean real competition. Any woman who knew anything would know he was *it*!

She put the first on and got herself a weak vodka collins, then laid on the sofa to watch.

What was that noise from the kitchen? It sounded like someone opening the sticky drawer.

There had damned well not be anyone in her condo! She'd have their ass in jail so fast they wouldn't know what hit them!

She got up and marched to the kitchen.

The light didn't come on. She could just make out a silhouette against the window over the sink.

"I don't know who you are or how you got in here, but you picked the wrong place this time!" she announced.

The figure turned toward her. Someone in a rain parka? What was that thing?

The figure moved toward her. She knew fear for the first time. She turned to run. The figure came close behind her.

What did...?


Det. Linda Birns, violent crimes, finished typing

out the report on that knife fight in the docks, printed out a copy, and put it in a file folder. She would keep it handy. This one wasn't over. That bunch had some kind of power play going on.

Det. Danny Betts, her sidekick on the six to two, put both their reports in the master file and came to draw a cup of the almost drinkable coffee from the urn. They discussed the power struggle among the dock people. Something had happened that made it critical, all of a sudden.

"The skuttle I've picked up says there's a missing shipment. Everybody's blaming every-body else," Danny suggested. "I say, let's be too busy somewhere else when we get the next call from down there. It's going to turn into a war. Let them kill each other off until we only have the one bunch to watch. We've made it plain enough that we'll stay out of it if they keep it there and no honest Joe gets drawn in."

Linda shook her head. "I would go along with that to an extent if the suggestion hadn't come from where it came from. If a politician gets involved, watch out! There's a big slime pond forming!"

The 9-1-1 line lit. It was transfer, so it would be real and for them.

"Betts. Violent crimes. Yes?"

She wrote a few lines and shifted the call to the

desk for further information. Danny raised an eyebrow.

"DB. Female. Semi-society. Blooody. Head. Neighbor found. The Brightview Towers. Seven B."

Danny grabbed his jacket, she grabbed her bag, they headed for the car.

*Bloody Messes*

Linda slipped on the latex and went to where the CSI van was just unloading Millie Parsons and crew. They went to the door, where an older "fluffy" woman was sitting in a lawn chair with a small poodle on her lap. The woman said she was Jennifer Rankin, a neighbor. She had heard the stereo going a bit loud. The victim, Anne Milsap, usually didn't make noise. It wouldn't be bad if the door were closed. These places were well-constructed and had decent soundproofing. She found her there. Like that!

Danny would take a complete statement. She went to the body.

Anne Milsap had been somewhere between attractive and pretty, if that was a picture of her before getting that injury. The picture was on the table just to the left as you entered. It was Milsap and some man. This was an expensive area, she had on expensive clothes. A look inside the condo showed she didn't skrimp on much. It just missed being to the point of ostentation.

Her head was split almost in two. It was one bloody mess.

Millie came to inspect the body. Linda led the CSI team inside. They said this one probably wouldn't have anything direct and immediate inside. She went to the door and got an axe to the head as soon as she opened it.

Linda agreed. She went in to take her own set of pictures, then went to look for anything on the surface. Milslap had a lot of pictures of herself with different men. The men tended toward the jock type. Linda thought of men's reputation for notching the headboard. This looked like Milsap's scorecard. These pictures were there for her girlfriends to be jealous over.

There was a datebook on the dresser in the bedroom. Linda bagged it with a special label. Millie would know what extra processing she wanted. There didn't seem to be a diary, which didn't fit the psychology of anyone who would keep that picture gallery. Millie would find it.

After a thorough search of the bedroom Linda went out and to the kitchen. Danny was covering that. He wouldn't miss an inch. They both knew the bedroom and kitchen were the important places when the victim was female. Millie would cover it all. She wouldn't miss anything. She was good!

She was going out to inspect the area around the door where Millie would have already done a much better job than she could. Her radio signaled, then she got a report of another dead body in the area. Top of the Hill Condos. Female. Wealthy socialite. Body in private garage area, found when maid was going home. Scene secured.

Danny got the same call, so they headed for the car. She called that Millie would have a lot to do tonight. Millie called that she got the same call they did. Fifteen minutes. She would leave their expert there for the computer part.

In today's world, there was often a lot more information on a computer than anywhere else. Both she and Danny had noted the laptop on the charger in the living room.

"I thought the war would be down on the docks, not up on the hill," Danny said sourly. She gave him the finger.

Ginger Parker had an almost exact injury. A bloody blow that cut the head almost in half. She was in the top condo of the top condos. That twelve ninety five rain slicker she probably paid a thousand bucks for and the obvious Guchi and D'Or etc. acoutrements said she had more money than anyone had any use for. Linda thought she wasn't attractive, so made up for it with the designer crap. Just a glance around at the Jaguar and the BMW and the Viper said most of what needed saying.

Carole Dinsmore, the maid, said she was not hard to work for, but she would never lower herself to being a friend with an employee. She hadn't liked other women and she didn't really like any of the men she dated. That was all for social position and whatever. Her life was one big pose. She didn't feel anything. She and all those society women she ran around with were all the same. Empty was about as good a description as she could come up with.

So she resented the type. It came with the job. The job paid double what she could get anywhere else, so smile your empty smile and act like an idiot for the royal ... royal.

She would like to see someone slap Miss Ginger around until her teeth rattled, but she didn't want anyone to actually hurt her. She couldn't help being what she was. It was how she was raised after being born with a lack, with something missing in her mental makeup.

Linda gathered a lot of information by commiserating with the household help when the lady of the house was of the type. All this would be solidified in the investigation, but she had a good workable base to understand a lot about Ginger Parker.

Danny checked over the Jaguar and the other cars. Linda checked over the area. Millie came in the van. She called the standby crew to come in. She didn't like the feel of this. At all! The kind of killing had a lot of rage and/or hatred behind it. It was very rare for this kind of thing to be only two.

They started checking over the condo. It was *very* expensive, but tasteful. Not the ostentatious type. The place looked almost like it could be comforatble – to an extent.

The third call. Millie got it at the same time, of course.

"Told you so!" she said. "At least they're close. All on the hill."

Linda sighed and said she'd bet she didn't get to sleep for another fifty hours, at this rate.

Danny was at the car. He didn't say anything. He would drive this one.

Gladys Roth, semi-wealthy socialite. Sungold Condos. Found by maintenance man. Carbon copy story. All were the type half the people were neutral about and half had a gripe, but it didn't seem the type who had enemies who would go nearly so far. Any real insight into their lives meant most would tend to pity them. The hatred would be to the extent of Carole. You'd like to see them get a smack in the puss. You wouldn't want them actually hurt.

Obviously, this didn't apply to everyone.

Barbara Lakehurst was found in the morning. Same MO, same mess, same type, same most everything. Hopefully, that would be all for awhile.

Linda sat at her desk with the copies from CSI and her own pictures and notes. Danny same at his desk. Other than sordid lifestyles, what was the common denominator here?

MO = axe to the head. Messy. Emotional. Rage and/or hate.

Pictures from victim's collection.

"Linda, look for others in that group who are the same type, but who didn't get an axe to the head," Danny suggested.

Linda nodded. That was a foregone, but it was a good time to look at that. It could save another trip through the same things.

"Look for men they all dated," she suggested. They did this with each case. Reminded each other to save steps.

They listed what they found on the computers, then would compare notes later. In several earlier cases this resulted in that one little item that connected other items.

Time, early evening to mid-evening. Rain.

Was the rain an important factor? Did this happen at this time because the rain caused changes in plans or patterns?

What did they know about the attacker? The method suggested male, but that wasn't even close to a definite. The weapon made it very unlikely they could tell anything about the physical characteristics of the killer.

There were no other clues. No one saw anyone around. No one heard anything. There would definitely be splatter from that, but it was during a rainstorm, so the killer possibly – probably – was wearing a raincoat that could be washed or disposed of.

Linda studied Millie's conclusions and theories. More would come from the autopsies, but they couldn't expect much.

*From the depth of the wound and the resistance factors, from the width of the cuts, I would suggest a standard type of wood axe. If longer handle, lighter axe or weaker attacker. shorter handle with heavier axe and/or stronger attacker. some evidence of righthanded attacker, but indefinite. Single blow in all cases. As noted, rage or hatred.*

Not much.

Diary in Ginger Parker case. That could be a break.

Linda went through the evidence to find the diary in its baggie. It had been printed and tested in several ways. There was nothing except what was written in it. There was a note that it had been scanned in entirety. She could return the diary to evidence and get copies.

Danny called that there were a lot of memory sticks plus the HD copies. They all had computers. He would spend a few hours seeing if there was something on that. He had official copies, so the stuff could be returned to the evidence room. Linda agreed and Danny took all the stuff back except their copies.

They had coffee and divided the items. This would be the borrriinngg part of it.

It had to be done. They got to it.


They all kept diaries. Linda had mentioned that they were all the psychological types who would. Danny agreed. The diaries were on the computers. It would be the break that could make a case for them.

They would look for the obvious. Danny had a framed page on the wall he took from a SF book he read when in school. They had found it to often be the way to go in their cases.

*"When all else fails, look at the obvious"*
*"All he did was see the obvious! - What more did any genius ever do?"*
"Danny, let's do a quick go-through. List names

and dates. Nothing else."

"Yo!"

They spent more than two hours on that one. Each had a list of from forty seven to a hundred thirty nine names and dates.

"Okay. Now let's correlate to find the names all of them listed."

They had twenty eight names mentioned over a period of four years.

"Danny, last two years, if not mentioned ... last two years. This one wouldn't wait more than a few months, at most. Men they actually dated, not that were mentioned as being at a party or something."

"Yo!"

They had eight names plus one that raised a question.

"Linda, I'm going to check out this Gary Sandersohn. They all mentioned him, but none of them actually dated him. They went to dinner or a show, but always with others. He wasn't a date. I want to see why he was ... oh. Here it is. Parker originally introduced him. He's an actor. He's gay. They all confided in him. He gave them makeup tips and showed them how hairstyles ... and that.

"You know Harry, in bunko. He's a guy every-one likes, but he makes no secret of the fact he's gay. You women get his advice about that kind of thing."

"He showed me where my hair style didn't quite fit my face. I look a hundred percent better with this one. He wouldn't kill a cockroach ... well, he can be pretty tough, as he's proven. He's one of the three cops I know who were in actual shoot-outs. He saved Wilma's ass in that. He broke a goon's neck for him."

"So. Who do we have? We can each take four and go through everything to see who turns up.

"I did note two names that came up with all of them. Two people none of them liked, so that was more than likely equal."

"Kilian Marks and Nancy Preston. I'll take Kilian, you take Nancy."

"Yo! I'll have her, Frank Breston, James Sinclair, Robert Wing, and Paul Sikes."

"I have Nancy, Earl Fields, George Thomas, Silvio Perez, and Vince Udahl. After lunch. It's already one twenty."

Danny saluted and put the evidence in neat stacks on his desk. Linda did the same, then they went to Lucy's Home Cooking, just two blocks away, for a late lunch. They went back to the station and to their desks. It was three hours later when they had all they were going to get. It was a lot, and it was nothing. They had noted each mention, then had cross-indexed each thing mentioned.

They compared notes. Nothing jumped out from the page.

"Okay," Linda suggested. "We're on regular shift in an hour. I'll take my list and try to find where everyone was last night." Danny nodded.

First would be Kilian Marks. He had addresses for all of them. She was in the Grandview Residential Hotel. He went to find she wasn't home. The desk man said she was on a plane for Los Angeles as of four thirty yesterday afternoon.

Shorter by one.

Linda used the same logic on Nancy Preston, who lived in a large fancy house just outside of town. She was a little plump and somewhat coarse-featured. She had been home last evening. It was raining. She didn't leave the house on that kind of night. The house manager would verify.

The house manager, Rodrigo Valdez, said that she was, so far as he knew, in the entertainment room, watching a movie, when he left at seven thirty.

Was that a pointed "So far as I know?"

No elimination there!

Danny's next was Frank Preston. He lived near the lake, but not on the shore. He was just short of in the wealthy area. He was an affable handsome man, bodybuilder type. He was a semi-gigolo. He spent the evening with Andrea Wright. A quick check found he actually did. Two less suspects.

Earl Fields was a ruggedly handsome jock type. Linda usually was repulsed by the type, but he seemed open and honest. He spent the evening with Florence Quentin, second apartment to the left. She confirmed. One possibility and one elimination.

James Sinclair was a slickly handsome man with impeccable taste in clothes and food. He had enough income that he could enjoy the best of both. Danny didn't much care for him and his snobbish attitude, but that had nothing to do with his job. He was with a lady he wouldn't name. A gentleman didn't.

One who would remain on the suspect list.

Linda asked George Thomas, another jock type, where he was last night. He said he heard about the murders.. Before eight o'clock, he was there. After, he was with Loyd and Eva Gregory. A party at their house. Kyle Kohnrad was there. One of the murdered women, Barbs Lakehurst, was supposed to meet him there, later. Robert Wing was supposed to meet someone there. He didn't know if it was one of the murdered women.

Wing was a suspect on Danny's list. She called. He hadn't checked. She said he was at a party with another man who was supposed to meet Barbara Lakehurst there. Two off the suspect list.

That left Paul Sikes for Danny's list. He lived across the lake from Preston. He wasn't home, but a neighbor said he would be at Tim's Tall Tail, a local little club where a lot of people spent time.

Danny found the club and went in. Sikes was a very likeable type. He was with friends, two right there tonight. He introduced Henry Overton and Fred Yale. They spent a lot of time at The Tail, playing pool and chatting. Danny met Gary Sandersohn, who was a jock type and not in the least effeminate. They had a beer and chatted. Danny would consider this an off-duty hour, seeing he had worked all day.

James Sinclair was the only one on his list who remained on his list.

Linda found that Silvio Perez had been at four different bars. That didn't eliminate him. He had plenty of time between bars, all of which were in that area.

Vince Udahl had been at the Country Club by the lake with three people.

Landa called Danny, who said he was heading back to the station. He only had one possible. Linda said she had two, so the list was shorter by six. Progress!

Later, just before they checked out, Linda wrote

*James Sinclair, Nancy Preston, Silvio Perez* on the little chalkboard. They would come in at one tomorrow to see which one they could prove did it, so they could close this one out!

Danny smirked and gave her the finger. This would probably turn out to be one of those things that took five years to solve, if they ever did. Linda laughed.

"We can do the rest of this crap together. I didn't get any real feelings about any of them on the list. I don't think our perpetrator is on the list," Linda complained.

"Take them in that order?" Danny pointed at the chalkboard. Linda shrugged. They took their own notes about Sinclair and went to the nearby places he might have frequented. He didn't frequent any of them. The one where he was known at all, The Eagles Nest, the bartender said he stayed at the country club by the lake or in the hill places. He wasn't the type to be slumming at regular bars.

Linda and Danny didn't fit the country club scene. It was their job. Danny used it to advantage when he suggested to the stiff shirt at the entrance that they could speak somewhere in private with employees, or they could come with a court order and hold the questionings very publicly, or they could take the bunch of them in to the court, where the judge would order them to answer questions for the record. His choice. It could take a few minutes or a few hours. Also his choice.

"After all, we're investigating the murders of

four of your clients. I'd think you'd very much want that solved," Linda finished for Danny.

"Er, um, well, of course, that is. We, ah, um, yes. Perhaps the, er, the changing room for the employees, er, behind the, um, the kitchen, you see."

"We'll have to ask a very few questions of the people who worked in the restaurant and bar the night of the murders. This is to eliminate people as suspects, not to accuse anyone," Linda answered. "We don't have any suspects among the employees, and no serious suspects among the clientele. This is mostly routine. After all, if a person was working here or seen here, they are no longer on any suspect list. We might have a couple we will want to warn to be careful. They may become victims of an axe murderer if we can't solve this quickly."

He looked shocked. Danny noted that, and a little fear, so added, "It's to protect the employees, to a great extent. What if you or someone else here knows something dangerous to a killer – and you aren't aware you have that information? Would you be at risk to insure your silence?"

He looked like he would faint. Linda was glad she was on the other side of the starched shirt. She couldn't quite hide the look that said, plainly,

"Right in the gut, huh?"

"Eegh? Er, we will cooperate in any possible way! This is such a terrible thing! This can't be happening among the people of class ... I mean, it is something from a horror movie!"

"If we could ask you a few questions, then the people who worked that night, then we'll be gone, hopefully, with a lot of people no longer in danger," Linda said.

"Yes! Of course! If I know something I don't know I know, and you find it, it will no longer be necessary to silence me! That is true! It is for our safety! You know your job. It is a thing that would never occur to the average working person!"

"*Our job is to protect* isn't just a slogan on the cars," Danny replied. "We take it very seriously."

"Miss Ames! Front, please!"

A pretty woman in a skimpy white French Maid outfit came to look questioningly at him. "Mr. Andrews?"

"Yes. Please. Take the station while I try to aid our friends from the police. They wish to find the *axe murderer* who killed those four poor women!"

He waved toward the hall behind the desk. They followed him into a clean changing room. There were several chairs and a vanity they could use as a desk.

"We'll do this as quickly as we can," Linda said. "We need to know about your personal reactions to several people. The real suspects are among them, but people we know are innocent are included. If you happen to have information about someone, it will be obvious it isn't something you brought up. They would have no way to know who among you knew the fact.

"I'll throw names at you. If they were here the night in question, that eliminates them as suspects, assuming they stayed more than an hour.

"Nancy Preston? What do you think of her, and was she here?"

"Er, well, I don't like to give personal ... but that is important in this kind of thing, I suppose. I mean, gossip ... you must realize that much of what I may say is really from gossip.

"She was not here. I find her to be a most trying person. Demanding and condescending, you see. Other patrons say she is a, well, it is what they say, bitch. She has no class. It is sad that so many who have the wherewithall to become members are like that, you see."

Linda smirked slightly at Danny. Andrews was a gossip. She would play to that. He could tell them a lot, but they would have to check it out.

Too much would be personal.

"Oh, I know!" she commiserated. "I've had to interview a couple who were, well, shall we say, had their noses so high in the air they would drown if it rained!"

He rolled his eyes. "If you only knew! The things that we have to handle 'with discretion' would show the world what kind of pig stye this place can be!

"Please don't get me wrong, but *some* of these people are just plain disgusting! Pilars of the community! Crooks and worse! I *know*!"

"James Sinclair?" Danny said, before he got on a rant.

"I see you weren't just shooting in the dark! The prime example of prime examples! I could tell you ... talk about a condescending bastard! If it wouldn't cost me my job, I could enjoy kicking his slimy ass! A millionaire, but a gigolo! He takes disgusting to new low levels!

"He was not here!" he finished, triumphantly.

Danny saw what Linda had been doing, so replied, "I hate to say it, but I almost prayed you wouldn't give him an alibi. Thank you, Jesus!"

"You know, he really did hit that Donlevy woman. I can't say she didn't ask for it, but a true gentleman would never consider hitting a woman, no matter the reason.

"We're not supposed to ever tell anyone about that, but this is about a *murder*!"

"No," Linda said. "It's about four murders *we know of*. All women a lot like Donlevy, I would say, wouldn't you?"

"Oh, yes. I would say that! The Parker woman and the Lakehurst woman were too much like her. Always trying to get into any man's pants any of the others of the type want. It's like some kind of contest with them. It's just plain sickening!"

"Paul Sikes," Danny said.

"Paul is a very nice person. He is one those women chase after all the time. He finds them, as he put it to me, like a bunch of bitches in heat. I don't think he would ever hurt anyone, much less kill anyone."

"Gary Sandersohn?" Linda asked. Danny was a bit surprised, but they did say they would throw in names they knew had no connections.

"He is a very nice person who will do anything to help others. I can't approve of his lifestyle, but must confess that I had a very disturbing experience with a homosexual when I was a teenager. It is something that is there, though I wish it were not. No other, certainly not Mr. Sandersohn, has ever done anything to me. He was not here ... well, maybe earlier for a very short time."

"Earl Fields?" From Danny.

"I do not know much about him. He seems a regular sort of person. He does exhibit some class, though some of his friends do not. He was not here."

"Kyle Kohnrad?" From Linda.

"Oh, please! The porno star? Really! Talk about someone who does not belong here! He was not here."

"Silvio Perez?" From Danny.

"I do not know the gentleman."

"Vincent Udahl?" From Linda.

"He was not here. He does come in sometimes, but I do not know the gentleman."

"Well, that covers most of what we need to know. I think you've said what you know about the victims. It's the general consensus among those we've spoken with," Linda said.

"If you will have Ames come in? She's closest right now, but I doubt she knows anything. Thank you. Everything here is confidential. You need not worry that anyone you spoke of will hear what was said," Linda said.

"I have little experience with the police. I was afraid it would be like those movie things, but you are just real people doing your job, aren't you?"

"We try to treat people the way we would wish

to be treated," Danny replied. Andrews went out.

Ames came in, looking a little embarrassed. She said not to judge anything about her from the uniform. The CEO of the place had less class than even some of the clients. He was from Nowhere, Central Texas, or something and thought French Maid was higher class than Cowgirl. If she could get as much working almost anywhere else, she would be out of there so fast it would make his head swim.

"Believe me, we know the type. All the bars down by the docks are run by Chauvinist pigs, even the ones that are run by women," Linda commiserated. "I worked as a waitress in a café just upside that was owned by one of the people who own bars down there. She expected the girls to be whores on the side, I think. As you said, as soon as I found a job that paid as much somewhere else, I was gone! I was going to the academy. I had to make enough to live on. It served as good experience when I got onto the force. I know how a lot of people we have to deal with think.

"What we'll do here is to throw names at you. Most of them aren't suspects, but we'll throw in the names of suspects, of course. You may know something you aren't aware of. It will, hopefully, come out.

"Everything is confidential. We aren't doing any other department's job. This is about four murders.

"Nancy Preston?"

"Bitch. Not here. Next?"

"She seems to be a lot like the dead women," Danny said. "Paul Sikes?"

"Nice enough. He wasn't here."

"Gary Sondersohn?" From Linda.

"He's a real pal. He helps all of us with makeup and hair styles and all that, but he's not the swishy type. He seems a lot more masculine than a lot of those gigolos. He's even pals with some of them, but he doesn't like others.

"He didn't like those dead women. He doesn't like pigs and bitches who play stupid games.

"He was here at five, when I came on. He left after a few minutes. We traded a joke about Sam Wentworth, the golf pro.

"Good-natured. He doesn't cut people down or anything."

"Kyle Kohnrad?" From Danny.

"What a worm! He makes slimy into almost an acceptable alternative. He thinks women will fall all over themselves when he walks into a room.

"Those four and several others do, but they don't feel anything. It's just competition.

"I saw one movie he was in. A bit part with a

woman in a bar. He couldn't act his way off of a down escalator."

"Robert Wing?" From Linda.

"Very nice. A little sold on himself, but with reason."

"James Sinclair?" From Danny.

"Snob. Not too bad. He wasn't here, I don't think."

"Silvio Perez?" From Linda.

"Don't know him. I've heard he's a good bed partner."

"George Thomas?" Danny.

"Really a nice enough person, if a bit formal. He doesn't come in much. He wasn't here."

"Earl Fields?" Linda.

"A dream, at times. A bit moody. Gorgeous to look at. He was here when I came on. I think he left about six or so."

"Vincent Udahl?" Danny.

"Please! He wasn't here. Jerkoff in spades."

"Kilian Marks?" Linda.

"Another pea in that pod. She's exactly what the four were. Not here."

They threw some random names at her. It didn't add anything.

Larry Hart, the bartender, said much the same as Andrews and Ames. The four other waitresses said about the same, though one thought Udahl was misunderstood. He was really alright. One said she had dated Kohnrad. He was about as good in bed as he was an actor, with nowhere to go but up, and he didn't have it in him to go up.

Linda and Danny went to the car to sit to list what they had.  They ended up with:

K. Marks – a ditto of the dead women. Out.

N. Preston – another ditto, but also ugly. In.

F. Breston – out.

J. Sinclair – jerk. In.

R. Wing – reg. Out.

E. Fields – nice guy. Out.

G. Thomas – nice guy. Out.

S. Perez – ??. In.

V. Udahl – jerk plus. Out.

K. Kohnrad – slimepit. Out.

G. Sondersohn – Gay. Friends w/all. Prossibly in, possibly out. Motive?

"Well, it looks like we're down to two definitely in and two possibly in," Linda said. "We proceed.."

"We have to look at each one of those four. We have to do it together, one at the time," Linda decided. "Danny, let's try to establish a motive, other than competition. The diaries might give us something. We have that on two, so let's eliminate them, if we can. I don't get a feeling. I don't like either one, so keep a thumb on me."

"I don't like them, either. We have to keep personal feelings out of it. They're both names on a list. That's all."

They took what they had about Nancy Preston to Linda's desk and sat. Linda brought up what she had on the computer. They merged what Danny had about her and ran it to list.

N. Preston, F. 27. Msmrph. Wealthy. Drives. Travels. Empty (that was their personal feelings. It was a personality and psychological point). +cmptv. SPRD. (The sexual predator fit, as they'd both known, both women and men.)

*An ugly woman who uses makeup and padding to make herself more attractive. Depends on wealth to get what she wants. Border sociopath. A possibility, but 2 nos.*

"So. She goes to a few places, but mostly stays in that ostentatious mansion. Neither of us think she did it," Danny said. "Let's see if we can find her favorite haunts and ask a few questions. The least it will do is eliminate one more suspect.

"Linda, why is Sondersohn on this list?"

"I think only because his name comes up everywhere. I like him. I only spoke to him a few minutes once, but he's really a nice guy.

"I don't have him on the list as a true suspect. He wouldn't have motive, but I think he might know a lot of things we can use. He knew them all. He went to the same places a lot of the time. A lot of the gay crowd gossip enough that he would know hundreds of little things about hundreds of people."

Danny nodded. He felt that Sondersohn was somehow involved, though from an angle they hadn't considered. Their hope was that he had the one fact that would tie this one around the killers' neck!

Linda sighed heavily. "Well, the diary will give us the places. Maybe a name or two from those places. Let's get at it. I want to solve it before Saturday night. I have a date. This kind of thing has a habit of intruding at the most inopportune times!"

Danny gave her the finger. She laughed.

They spent half an hour finding places and names from the diary. They were lucky that Preston didn't go to a lot of places.

"Lakeview, we've covered. Eagle's Nest has come up before. LeGrand Club, Hightower, and Frederique's. That should be easy enough. Let's check on the others, meaning Marks, to see which places both frequented," Linda suggested. "What's this?" She took a paper from he "In" file.

It was a coroner's report. Lakehurst was two months pregnant.

"So? In that strata, it would be handled by a trip to her doctor and never mentioned again," Linda said.

"Unless she wanted to use it ... Linda, she wouldn't be pregnant unless she fully intended to be. This adds quite a bit to the pot."

Linda thought for a moment. She said maybe blackmail – but not for money?

Danny nodded. "Frederique's is the only one likely before eight or so. We can hit there, then go home for a little rest. Meet at LeGrand at eight or so."

Linda's turn to nod. They went to the car, to Frederique's. They didn't learn much there. All the dead women spent some time there. It was a fancy place where fashions and such were shown and champagne was served. People went there to be seen. The prices were purely ridiculous. Fifty dollars for a glass of rather ordinary champagne?

Each to his or her own.

The LeGrand was an exclusive club. That Linda and Danny didn't fit was obvious. After all, his suit didn't cost a thousand dollars and neither did her dress. She wasn't wearing fifty thousand dollars worth of jewelry and wasn't driving a Lamborgini. He didn't have a top of the line Rolex and wasn't driving a Maseratti.

They were not members. Please don't block the drive. There were places down by the docks they would be welcomed.

Danny flipped open his wallet and showed the badge. "Look at the license plate. We go in and mingle to get the information we need or we come back with the squad and raid the place. Your call."

"I need the warrant, not a badge. I suppose you will have to bring the squad. Commissioner Felding is, I believe, vice president of the club?" the punky guard said, with a raised eyebrow and a sneer.

"As I said, your call!" Danny replied. He looked up a number from the police list and called. He was given a roaming cell number, which he called.

"Morris? Danny Betts. I'm with Linda. We're at the LeGrand. The asshole punk here says you're a vice president or something, so he knows I won't bring a squad and raid the place."

"We have to get some information about two people who come here. We're trying to eliminate suspects. This makes them even more suspect by a big margin."

"We'll be as discrete as possible. We're not in uniform, but that won't mean much in a place like this. We *are* in an unwanted uniform!"

Danny laughed. "I couldn't afford to have it cleaned on a cop's salary. I don't make enough in year to pay the interest on the loan to buy anything like that! It's an unmarked Honda, not even a Viper!"

He passed the cellular to the guard, who was actually sweating. He listened, then asked that they park to the left behind the gates to avoid the valet, who would give them a lot more trouble. Linda said they were used to it, but didn't want to cause any scenes.

They parked and went to the massive carved mahogany doors and inside, where a man in a tuxedo with a snobbish attitude held a hand out to demand their membership cards. The phone in his little podium rang. He ignored it. It rang again. Linda said he would show good sense to answer that one.

He sniffed and answered it, looked a bit scared, and waved for them to pass.

They went into a large room where people were walking around, talking in little groups – that became silent as they approached, then resumed as they passed.

The pretty women and handsome men who were carrying around trays of drinks and aperitifs avoided them.

A rather tall, boisterous woman, came to slap Linda on the back and announce, "I wish I had the balls to look like a human being in a place like this. I'm Lucy Stafford, Austin, Texas, oil and cattle and that kind of shit. Forty thousand acres of flat cow pasture and no cows, there.

"I like you already, and haven't met you! Doesn't occur to this bunch of phony clowns that you have as much or more than they do or you wouldn't get past the gate, sure as hell not inside!

"Tonight's going to be fun! You're real people, I'm real people, the rest are wannabe people.

"This crap they call champagne is just that. Crap! They have ... I guess you would know!

"What's your handle?"

"I'm Danny. She's Linda. We like to think we're people. I like you! I wish this was Texas and we were at a little bar I know, close to Austin City

Limits. Happy Knight. Real people and musicians and hillbillies and punk rockers and really awful poets.

"And fun! People here talk quiet and are so serious you could puke. We like to have fun in a place. We decided that's exactly what we'd do. Screw the phony crap! The only people they impress are people just like them – and who cares about them?"

"You want to know the truth? We came in a Honda! The guard shit in his pants, but he had to let us in. We parked behind the gate so no one would see it!" Linda said, with a giggle in her voice.

"Honey, I like you! I really like you!

"You're dressed for what we call 'slumming' in Texas. I think you can pull it off! Let's go to my place ... to the Target Store. I want to buy a nine ninety five outfit. We can go to the local places and act like we're real people. I just knew this was going to be a fun night when you walked in. I saw Jeeves' snob act, and he answered a call, and waved you through. I think he actually fainted after you were in!"

Linda gave Danny a look. He was already playing to this situation. They were both good at that. Lucy was the type who would know everything about everybody. "Let's do! Oh,

Danny, let's be what we really are for tonight! Please!"

"You're on! First one who mentions money or cars or yachts or that shit gets out, wherever we happen to be! Deal?"

They did a high five all around. Lucy put her glass on a passing tray and waved at the door. They went out. Lucy had a chauffeur and limousine waiting.

"Ah-ah! Honda!" Linda demanded.

"Take the rattletrap home. I'll be there when I get there," Lucy ordered, then waved at the Honda. They went to get in and drove away. Danny was driving. He headed down toward the Target Store, where Lucy went in in several thousand dollars worth of clothes and came out with a paper sack full of that and wearing a twenty two dollar outfit. She handed Danny a sack with over a million dollars worth of jewels in it. He tossed it into the console and they headed out for a night of fun.

They would get a lot of information before the night was over. Lucy would stay a friend. They were going to tell her the truth when they got to know each other a bit.

The Wheelhouse was a little bar close to the docks. It was popular, and there was seldom trouble there. It was a meeting place for dock workers and deckhands. There was loud music and prostitutes and whatever else.

Lucy said she finally found a place like home! She flirted with several men.

After about half an hour, when she said she had found heaven, Linda told her they were cops and that she knew she had found a soulmate in Lucy. She had been dreading having to stay at the LeGrand among that bunch of phonies. Lucy asked about homicide, said they had exciting lives, and that they were real people. She liked them. She would like to be buddies, to be able to go to regular places. The way she was raised was like this. She had married an old man who was a big name in oil and ranches. He had been killed when there was an explosion at one of the wells. She had a life she hated since then – until now.

She was attractive and had a great personality. She said she might actually take up one of the men who were flirting with her. They were, at least, men, not puppets on a social string.

"I haven't had a lover who could keep me awake, much less excite me, for three years. Tonight's the night!"

With that past them, Lucy gave them a lot of information about a lot of people. She wasn't spitefull or vicious. She said what she thought, which was pretty much what everyone else thought about The Bitch Club, as that bunch were called.

She went home with a man who Linda said made her wonder if a fling would be a good way to end the night. Lucy would come to the station in the morning for her stuff. She had never been in a police station before. It would be fun.

She did manage to eliminate both Marks and Preston as suspects.

Lucy came in just before noon. She said last night was probably the best night in her life. Danny said he'd forgotten the stuff and went to the car to get her clothes and jewelry. Linda introduced Lucy to the people at the station. She was a hit, being totally unexpected.

Linda said she had a date Saturday night. Lucy could get one, herself, and they would go to the stadium for the concert. Country and light rock. Four bands, semi-wellknown. Fifteen bucks a person to get in. Beer was two dollars. No hard booze.

"Hank will love that! We really hit it off, more than the sex, which was fantastic! I haven't been anyplace it cost fifteen dollars to get in in more than ten years! Fifteen hundred, lots. Two dollars for a beer? Not two hundred? Wow!"

Linda hugged her and said it was a date.

Now for the next one on the list. It was cut to

half. Neither Danny nor Linda thought the killer
was on that list, but it was part of the routine.

James Sinclair. 29. M. Msmrp. Body builder type. Snobbish and condescending. Wealthy.

They got out at the condos and went to number twelve B, a penthouse. The valet said he knew of no reason Mr. Sinclair would be involved in anything the police would take interest in, so perhaps they could find another place to spend their afternoon?

"Four of Mr. Sinclair's close friends have been murdered. Maybe we're here to prevent the same thing happening to him?" Linda said, sweetly. "Maybe you'd prefer to cause us to get a court order to have Mr. Sinclair hauled before a judge and made to testify in public about a lot of personal things?"

"I do not believe any such thing will happen. I will ask Mr. Sinclair if he wishes to speak with you."

He closed the door in their faces.

"I see he takes lessons in shitty attitudes from his boss," Danny remarked. "I think I *will* get a warrant and have him hauled in when he refuses to talk to us."

"I'll call the warrant request in right here where ratface can hear me. See if that enhances his job opportunities."

The door opened. The valet said that Mr. Sinclair was busy. He didn't have time to waste talking to police about things he had no interest nor connection with.

Linda took out the walky-talky and said, "Station eight. Fourax case. James Arthur Sinclair. Open court testmony about facts. Material witness. Reluctant. Will remain at this address until warrant and officers arrive. Form is on my desk, Bill. I expected this from him."

"Ten four. Williams is on this one. He'll sign, and the officer and warrant will be there in about forty minutes. I'll send the wagon. That should impress the neighbors."

Linda clipped the walky-talky on her shoulder strap and smiled at the valet, whose eyes were open wide in disbelief.

"Maybe you should have him get dressed in something appropriate for testimony in court," Danny suggested. "His attitude will go a long way toward deciding the kinds of questions he'll answer."

He and Linda turned their backs on him and went to the elevator. He went back inside and closed the door.

"Let's go sit in the lobby and have a cup of coffee or something until the warrant gets here," Linda suggested. Danny said he would be by the garage entrance. Sinclair drove a black Mercedes or a dark blue BMW.

Fifteen minutes later, Danny came into the lobby with Sinclair. "Fleeing to avoid court ordered appearance. Good for ten days, then extended to three months when he pulls the superior act in front of Judge Williams."

"Bill is bringing the warrant. We'll add this when we get to court. I'm sure Williams will be impressed, but not quite the way our detainee would prefer," Linda replied.

"But I don't know what you're talking about!" Sinclair cried. "I was simply going to my regular doctor's appointment! What court order? I don't know what's happening!"

"Oh? Your butler didn't bother to tell you we were going to have you hauled into court if you didn't answer a few questions here?" Linda snarled. "Give it up! We don't have time in a murder investigation to put up with this crap!"

"Yeep! Murder investigation? Gene told me ... but Gene only said two police came to ask questions and he sent them away! He didn't say anything about a court order! I would never refguse to answer questions about anything! My

God! This is crazy!"

"Yeah, right! And you didn't...." Danny began.

"Wait a minute! Your butler didn't say ... tell me exactly what he did say," Linda demanded.

Danny looked thoughtful. Maybe they finally had a definite suspect in this! "The butler did it!" wasn't always a joke ending to a case!

"He came in. I was in the gymnasium. I always do a short session before I go to the doctor's office. He said two police officers wanted to ask me some questions about ... he didn't say. I got the impression there were thefts in the building or something.

"Anyhow, he said he informed you that I certainly had no connections with anything so sordid. He said you left."

"He didn't come back to tell you we had ordered a warrant to have you testify in court as a hostile material witness?"

"My lord! No! He just said it was time I went to Dr. Phillips."

"Answer a few questions here, and I'll negate the warrant when it gets here," Linda promised. "You have to be aware of the four axe murders. Where were you that night?"

"It was raining. I stayed in. I was in the entertainment room. I fancy myself as more than adequate a pianist, and was practicing some

Chopin. Polanaise."

"Where was your butler?"

"I haven't the vaguest. It was his night off. He has family somewhere close, I believe."

"Did you date Barbara Lakehurst much?"

"A few times. She and I didn't have any particular affinity, if you know what I mean."

"Were you aware she was pregnant?"

"Barbs? No. She would have that taken care of in ten minutes. She wouldn't be preg ... so she was trying to get a hold on someone. It would be Earl or George. That would fit what she was."

Linda nodded. "We sort of felt...!"

Danny exclaimed, "Doc! I have to get in touch with Doc. Now!"

He used the walky-talky to call the ME station. It took about five minutes to reach Dr. Walters.

"Doc? Danny Betts. DNA samples from the fetus. Lakehurst. You have them?"

"Because the half match will tag the killer. I'll try to get samples from several people. Anyone who refuses will take a lot of looking at. Thanks, Doc."

He turned to Sinclair. "Would you offer a DNA sample?"

"Certainly!"

Linda went to the car for swabs and phials. Danny asked if there was anything in the apartment they could use to get a sample from the valet. Sinclair thought for a minute, then said he would get a good sample! Gene cut himself in the kitchen and threw the bloody bandage in the trash. It was still there!

Danny waited until they had the sample from Sinclair and called in to cancel the warrant request, then they rode up in the elevator to the penthouse. The valet didn't answer the door. Sinclair used his key card and they went in. The trash had been dumped into the incinerator bin.

"Oh, double damn! What do we do! I have a *murderer* in my employ!"

"Not definite, but likely. He stayed here?"

"Yes, except the one night per week. The room behind the kitchen."

They went to the room. Danny used a penknife to open the door. The room had been spotlessly cleaned.

There was an ashtray with several used tooth-picks in it.

"Oh, yes!" Sinclair cried. "I saw those CSI things on TV! Toothpicks are as good as swabs – and no one else has been in this room for more than four years! That test will certainly as sunset show his DNA pattern! He won't get away from this now!"

"Change the keycard code on all entrances to

this place. Now!" Linda demanded.

"Oh! My God! Yes! Certainly!"

"Don't go anywhere alone," Danny warned. "Does he have his own car?"

"He uses the BMW or the Mercedes. I have the Mercedes downstairs, so the BMW will be gone."

"Not far!" Linda said. She made an APB call for the car. She thought for a minute, then said, "Danny will drive your car to the doctor's office. You can ride with me. He could be waiting for you there, but I think he won't be after you."

"I suppose not. This is very exciting, in a negative way."

Sinclair went to the office and said to immediately change all the lock codes in the place. Do not give the new cards to anyone except him. Personally. Face-to-face. Do not trust Eugene McCall, for any reason, at any time.

Then they headed for the cars.

They found the BMW at the MacDonald's a mile and a half away. Eugene Francis McCall was not there. The APB was changed to him. Sinclair gave them a picture and SS number and such from his employment records. McCall had a pistol permit, so there was another way to locate him. The pistol wasn't in the room, so he had it with him. That made him A&D.

Danny took the work records to copy on the machine in the den at Sinclair's. He found Sinclair wasn't as bad as he seemed from second-hand information, which still didn't make him any prize. He was cooperating in all ways.

An idea: He called in to ID with all the information he had on McCall. He found the pistol permit was revoked because he had tried to carry it into a bank. He'd claimed he had forgotten he had it on him and was provisionally revoked. Another month and it would be re-instated unless there was anymore negative information about him.

He had no police record in the state. He was from Oregon, so his home town was checked.

Penning. He was a bit of a tough growing up. He had a couple of minor arrests when he was a teenager. He was once under suspicion of armed robbery, but it was not found one way or another, and there had been no more arrests for anything except a rape charge that was found to be baseless. She was a prostitute he didn't pay was what reading between the lines told him. The police have their own way to code such things into the record without actually stating them. "Angeline Fremont charged that she was forced into various sexual acts over a period of two weeks. She had met McCall in the Blue Light Bar and thought they had a mutual attraction. McCall took her to his apartment, where she found she was expected to offer her sexual favors to someone who cared. It was three o'clock AM and there was no one else about. She couldn't resist him, as he is quite strong. The next incident was two nights later. It was much the same. She had a few drinks (regularly) and found herself in the same situation. She had reported similar incidents in the past."

It went on. What it said to other investigators was that she worked the bars, went home with a John at three in the morning, slept with him, he didn't pay, but probably promised to pay when he got his paycheck. She went with him again and he didn't pay, so she brought the charges. She'd pulled that one before. Put it in the dead file.

McCall had worked as a personal valet for a mobster in Los Angeles before moving there. He was also a licensed OTR commercial truck driver. He had worked for a woman in Napa Valley for awhile, but was suspected of petty theft and was terminated. He worked for other women for short periods.

This had probably started with embezzlement from Sinclair or something such. He was also a bit of a gigolo, which was the connection with Sinclair. Maybe these women had all used him and were about to get his ass fried in his cushy job, which would let it out that he had been stealing from Sinclair.

Or something. Let the theories wait until they had more information. Until they had him. It shouldn't be long.

They called it a day and went home.

In the morning they looked up Silvio Perez. He was the Latin Lover type, but really not a bad person. He was born in Los Angeles, of Mexican parents. His father and mother were both bit part players who made decent money at it. They were both more than average attractive, and had talent. He was raised more in the American style. Linda could see the attraction of the women to him. His smile was definitely warm and ... inviting. He was quite handsome, in an overly smooth way.

They had almost the exact time of the Parker murder. He was in the bar at the Evening Breeze Hotel during the entire time he would have to have been at Parker's. He was off the list. Danny was half sure they knew the killer. Linda was almost three-quarters sure. Sinclair was out. He wouldn't have the ability to kill anyone in that manner. If it had been poison, he would be in it. It was a direct assault. He didn't have it in him.

"We have to hope McCall's it," Linda complained. "We don't have anymore suspects.

"Sinclair and McCall were not the father. We still have that to look at. It makes me a bit uneasy about McCall. He's running from something, but what? It might not have anything to do with our case."

"I'll spend some time looking for DNA samples. You have a date tonight. There's not anything else to do until we talk with McCall. I'm less and less convinced he's it."

Linda nodded. "We can let this ride until Monday unless something comes up. Maybe, if McCall didn't do it, the DNA will give us the answer. Trouble with that is that all our suspects there are absolved. It won't make sense unless we can show ... something.

"Danny, this might be the one that gets away from us."

"If he gets away with this, he'll get pissed at someone and do it again. We can try to prevent anything like that. Not much else."

Danny managed to get the DNA samples from Wing, Udahl, and Sikes. Each negative gave him a more sinking feeling.

Well, Monday might give them a break.

Sunday afternoon Danny got a call, They found McCall at a family friend's house. A narco undercover man located him when his buddy bought a bag of weed from a subject with him along. The squad broke in and arrested everyone, confiscated the pot and some coke and meth. He was officially identified at the station. His pistol was hidden under the bed (how original!) McCall was using. He would get away with having it because it was under permit, even though the permit was under suspension. He was not carrying it on his person.

Danny called Linda and they met at the station when McCall was brought in.

McCall was a bit of a thug, and looked it. He was sullen and refused to talk.

"You can sit there and remain silent – and be charged with four counts of heinous murder – or you can tell us where you were the night the four women were killed," Linda lectured. "Let me warn you. Not telling Sinclair why we were there, then running, puts you in one hell of a position. I can see you being strapped down for the injection. There's no way out of that if you're convicted.

"Ball's in your court."

"I didn't have anything to do with killing those broads! They weren't worth killing!

"Okay. The night they were killed. My night off.

"I was at Aunt Eva's until about nine, then went with Sammy Goins to the Moonlight Bar on twenty third for another hour, then back to the place where we were staying.

"I didn't run because of any murders. I thought that was a way he was trying to get me for the ... stuff. He's really kind of stupid about a lot of things. If he had half a brain he would check on why groceries for him and me were three or four hundred a week. Things like that.

"He has so much he doesn't miss a couple of thousand a month. I have more than forty thousand in the bank in four years. Duh! At a thousand a month with room and board? Duh! I dress better than he does, and I have ten pounds of gold stuff? Duh! What does he need? A map of where everything's buried?"

"He's not the brightest star in the galaxy,"

Danny agreed. "Give him twenty five thou back and say you're sorry you treated him like that, then get back to Oregon and we'll drop anything from our end – if your alibi chacks out.

"Deal?"

"You're okay. Deal. It will check out. I'd be a fool to lie about that."

They took him back to a cell. Danny called Sinclair and said McCall was running because he had enbezzled several thousand from him. He would get a lot of it back if he would drop the case. McCall was no killer. He would have to leave the state as part of the deal.

"I was suspicious a couple of times. Two hundred eighty dollars for food in a week?

"I knew prices keep going up. I spend more than that at a restaurant some nights, so didn't worry about it. I'll get some of it back, so no harm done. You've done that for me. I guess I don't really deserve it. Thank you, officers."

He hung up. Linda said, "We don't have a suspect anymore."

"We can hope the DNA tests will give us something."

"Yeah! Thanks, Pandora!"

"I don't know what you're talking about half the time. How was your Saturday?"

"Oh, just a little past fantastic. Lucy's a real pal.

I think her first night slumming has her a long-term relationship. Hank's a great guy, and he's sexy as all hell. I could go for someone like that! He really likes Lucy. He doesn't know anything except her husband died in an industrial explosion, and that he had cows and such in Texas."

"Well, tomorrow at ten. None of that crowd will be up and about before then."

"Yeah. Back to the grind."

Linda suggested that they take the list in order. They had some, so it shouldn't be a real problem.

F. Breston, Earl Fields, George Thomas, and Kyle Kohnrad. If one of them wasn't the father, they really were in a sticky spot.

Breston looked a little surprised and nervous, but gave them the swab. He asked what it was for. They said Lakehurst was pregnant. They were looking for the father.

"Barbs? Pregnant? You're joking, of course. What's it really about?"

"She really was. We figure the father was going to be pressured or something," Linda explained. "She wouldn't be pregnant by accident."

"I can picture her doing something for pressure on someone, but pregnant? That wouldn't be anything ... it doesn't make any sense, but she wouldn't be pregnant except by plan. She could be scheming.

"How long?"

"About two months."

"Then it couldn't be something on me. I'm not the father in that time frame. It's been closer to six months since we did anything together.”

They went to Kyle Kohnrad’s place because it was so close. He willingly gave them the sample and asked what it was for. They told him.

“I’m out on that one! I’ve had a vasectomy! Two years ago.”

Earl Fields was a little nervous. He asked what it was for. Landa explained that Lakehurst was pregnant. They were looking for the father.

“I see. It will be me or George Thomas. She’s been trying to pressure both of us into marrying her so she could gloat over the others. I could picture her as a mother. Talk about a mother from Hell!

“I could be wrong. Nature changes a woman when she becomes a mother. Some of them. I wouldn’t marry her, no matter what, but she would make life Hell for me. I wouldn’t let it bother me much. She didn’t realize her whole bunch would know exactly what she was doing. She was close enough to the deep end she might go over.

“To tell the truth, I didn’t feel a thing when they told me she was dead. Maybe a little surprise, but nothing real or very deep.”

They chatted a bit. He really seemed a nice enough person. He definitely didn’t kill anyone, but what if he were the father?

It wouldn't change the fact he had an unbreakable alibi. He didn't kill anyone.

George Thomas was much the same. They were back to no suspects. Danny looked thoughtful, then asked, "I want to discuss something that you might not want Linda to hear. It's damned personal and none of my business, but it could be very much a part of this."

Thomas replied, "Ask away. I live an open enough life that nothing will do me any real harm. I can't think of anything you could ask that wouldn't be known to people."

"It's about Gary Sondersohn."

Linda looked shocked. Thomas grinned. "A couple of times. He's really a very good person. He's capable of deep feelings, which none of the Bitches Club are or were. He cares about people. Nothing on a more than casual order. Communication, I suppose. He's the only man I've kissed in that kind of way."

"Thanks. I didn't know if your group would feel open about such things."

"I think he and Earl and maybe Silvio – Silvio Perez. He wasn't around us much, but he's a very nice person. Kohnrad would try, but I can't picture Gary giving such as him a second look. Bobby Wing, probably. Maybe Sikes, but that would be iffy. Vince would try, but wouldn't get anywhere.

"He knows all the people in our circle. He told me a lot of times that I wouldn't believe how scheming and downright evil those women are. They would talk to him like he was one of them. He even said a couple were jealous as Hell because they thought he was sleeping with the ones they were after. He could picture Kohnrad and Udahl and Sinclair with them, but not the rest of us.

"It's part of life. We all have lived through a lot of things. With Gary, it was always understood that we would be pitchers and he would be catcher. I guess it sometimes went a bit further, but that's also a part of life. He wouldn't push anyone into anything. Things would sometimes happen in the heat of the moment, so to speak."

"I see. I'll ask Earl about it. He'll be as open as you, I think."

"I can't picture Gary doing anything like that, but I can. If he did it, I'll do all I can in his defense."

"I think all of you would."

They talked a bit more, then headed back to Earl. Linda was quiet. Just before they got to Earl's, she said. "I didn't want it to be him. I really didn't. Shit!"

"I didn't, either. It's what we had left. He kept

coming up, sort of on the sidelines. He's the only one with no hint of an alibi, so far as we know. We can hope he has one. I won't mind not catching this one if he's out of it – and I've never met him."

They stopped at Earl's and asked him about Sondersohn. He said he guessed it was true that they were a lot closer than just friends. Gary was a very special person.

"George said he was always warning the lot of you about those women, that they were evil, scheming bitches. You wouldn't believe the truth about some of them."

"Danny, if he did it ... he did it for some of us. He shouldn't have. We know what's going on. We use it, at times. None of us feel anything about those women. We do about Gary. He wouldn't do anything like that for himself. It would be for us. Oh, God!"

"We can hope he has an alibi," Linda said.

"If he did it and we all swore he was with us and couldn't have, he'd admit it. He would never allow anyone to do that for him, even though he'd do it for us in a flash."

They talked a bit more. Linda and Danny said they'd better go to Sondersohn's. They would have to, sooner or later. Might as well get it over with.

They pulled up at Sondersohn's place and went up to the apartment. He met them at the door and invited them in.

"Come to arrest me?"

"Sorry. Yes," Danny replied. "You were expecting us?"

"Yeah. Earl and George called. They said they were going to swear I was with them, but you already know where they were. They would set someone up. Refuse to answer questions."

"And you said you wouldn't go along with it," Linda said.

"And leave them all under suspicion. No."

"George and Earl were not under suspicion," Danny pointed out.

"But others are. Or were."

"Why?" Linda asked.

"Because those four had a scheme where they would make life pure Hell for all the guys. The ones worth knowing, anyhow. Not all of us are."

"Why would even such as them want to do anything like that?" Linda asked. "I just can't understand the type. Of all of them, Lucy is the only one I could like, and we're pals. Close. She's a real person. She doesn't think much of that bunch."

"The Bitches Club. She was never in it. I like the Hell out of her. She would fit there like Kohnrad fits our bunch. Not even in the running. Why even the bitches put up with him, I can't figure."

"Gary, you just said something. 'Those worth knowing.' Those women weren't worth killing, as both George and Earl commented," Danny said.

"They were really pathetic excuses for human beings," Gary agreed. "If it weren't for other things, I'd let them live for as many years as they would, being empty shells with nothing inside. Kohnrad and Preston and Marks will live a long time, probably, and not know an honest minute in their lives.

"All those women were in their late twenties. They were about to become, to them, over the hill old hags. They didn't know why. They had a plan to force the guys into marriage so they wouldn't be alone. They didn't realize that would make them even more alone. They would be with a man who hated their rotten damned guts. They wouldn't dare to do anything that would give the man grounds. It would be a trap that they caught themselves in. If they had gone after Kohnrad and Sinclair and Udahl and maybe Breston, it would be a different thing. They were going after the decent ones. I wasn't about to let it happen.

"They had it set up to where they could pull it off. I know some things they had set up. It would turn your stomach. They would consider it a victory over each other as well as a victory in life. It would destroy four good people and themselves. There was no stopping it, so long as they were alive and scheming."

"Why an axe?" Linda asked.

"Milsap. I was going to strangle them. There was a fire truck at a filling station on the way. No one was there, and a fire axe was right there. I picked it up and went on. It hadn't been tied down, so they would think it dropped off in the road somewhere. If it was missed, they couldn't tie it to anyone.

"When she turned and saw me there with it, she knew the one moment of emotion in her sordid life. Terror!

"I decided that was going to be the way."

"It's messy."

"It was raining. I had on a rain coat. I could stand in the rain or under a gutter that was pouring and wash it off. Even the weather was with me that night. Sorry I left such a mess for you to clean up, but it's part of your job.

"Care for coffee and sticky buns? Might as well

not leave a lot of that crap around."

They sat at the kitchen table and chatted about all kinds of things, as well as the murders. Both Danny and Linda liked Gary. He was really a very nice person.

Even if he was an axe murderer.

They told him they would send a cop to arrest him in the morning. They didn't believe he would run. He could get some things together he would need and that would be allowed. He could arrange a good lawyer. They parted friends.

They went to the station, filed their reports, and went home.

In the morning they went in to hear their captain, Vern Morrow, throwing a fit because they had a statement drawn up to have an axe murderer sign when they brought him in.

"Why in hell didn't you bring him in last night? He'll be halfway to Rio by now!"

"He won't run. We didn't want to stay up all night for that crap. He did it. He admitted it. He explained it. We had coffee and sticky buns and said we'd have him arrested formally this morning. Good night," Linda explained. "What's the beef? We caught him."

"But no axe murderer is going to just wait for a cop to come arrest him! Damn it!"

"Captain Morrow, there's a man here to see

Betts and Birns. Says he decided to come in on his own, so we don't have to send anyone to pick him up. He said to tell you it's Gary, in case you have any other axe murderers to arrest this morning.

"Is this some kind of a joke? He's a dream walking!" Sgt. Sally Hern, desk, announced.

"Bring him in. He's gay, but you can try," Danny answered. Vern was standing there with his mouth open.

Gary came in with a suitcase and a paper bag. "I got some sticky buns. Same as last night. They're from the Donut Palace. They're as good as I've found.

"Do I check in my suitcase here, or at the jail, or what?"

"I'll get some coffee. It's pretty disgusting, but cop coffee is legendary for that," Linda said. "Put the suitcase by the desk. This is Vern, our captain, who said you'd be halfway to Rio by now."

"I didn't much care for Rio in the best hotels. I'll play the game by the rules, right here.

"Listen. Earl and George and who knows else will come in with alibis for me. They mean well. Don't charge them with false statements or whatever, okay?"

"I don't believe this is happening! I'm on some kind of trip! Somebody slipped some acid in on me, right?" Vern said.

They laughed. Linda brought them all coffee and Gary put the big plate of sticky buns on the desk. They all sat around and chatted, then sent Gary through processing. Everyone there liked him before that was done.

Several people came to try to give Gary an alibi. They said they had the confession, he had been processed, don't end up with perjury charges in a murder case. It could get them five years.

Linda and Danny went to the cells before they checked out to see how Gary was doing. He said he was fine. He liked most of the guys he would be spending the rest of his life with. Could they get the warden to put either four oh seven or three ninety eight in his cell? They joked awhile, then went home.

"Well, that came out better than I had hoped!" Linda said to Vern and Danny as they left the courtroom. "Minton was the perfect lawyer. If I'd been on the jury I would've insisted Gary get the citizenship medal!"

"I don't believe any of this actually happened. I really do like Gary, and I'm not easy on homos. He's different from the ones I knew growing up," Vern said. "When Minton came up with that spur-of-the-moment explanation for the axe, I couldn't believe it! Then he convinced the jury! Six years for four axe murders! I can't believe it!"

"If you'd been on the detail that investigated those women, you'd believe it," Linda said. "Everyone we talked to said they were the Bitches Club. They really weren't worth killing, and Gary really did believe he was protecting his friends. You heard them talk about him. He even made jokes for the jury, which didn't hurt a thing when they had to chose between manslaughter and murder one."

Lucy and Hank came over. They were going to the concert at The Grounds. Two heavy metal bands. Linda and Danny and dates were invited.

They chatted awhile. Linda would go to the concert. Danny would be on duty.

"I finally told Hank I was a millionairess. He said he wouldn't hold that against me until the first time I pointed out that I made more than he did, then he'd take an axe to me," Lucy said. "I don't think he really believes me."

"She is, but she doesn't let if screw up her life," Linda replied. "I wouldn't know what to do with that kind of life. I think I'd be like Lucy. To Hell with that phony crap! I'd want to be a real person, not a facade."

They went on, chatting and joking. Earl and George came to them. Linda said she had a date for the rock concert. Would Earl like to go?

"I've never been to a rock concert. I don't like that kind of music. Yes, I might actually enjoy it! I see Lucy found it's a better life than phony people in overdone phony places. If she likes hillbilly music, she doesn't pretend it's so far below her. She likes it and enjoys it. Maybe I could be human, too, if I work at it."

"If you work at it, it won't work. Let go and be yourself. Screw the world and it's silly conventions," Lucy replied. "Same rules as when we first met, right?"

"Damned right!" Linda answered.

"Rules, such as?" Earl asked.

"Mention money, planes, yachts, jewels, and you get tossed right there, wherever there is," Lucy said.

"You people get on with your rock concerts. Danny and I have to get back to work," Vern said.

They went their various ways. Life can be good if you let it.